veggies, smeggies

4 Penny, McKavity, Winnie, Cecil, Elaine and Bruno
On earth they are gone, but in our hearts they live strong

First published in 2006 by Simply Read Books
www.simplyreadbooks.com

Library and Archives Canada Cataloguing in Publication

Moore, Sean, 1976-

    Veggies smeggies / Sean Moore.

ISBN-10: 1-894965-41-8
ISBN-13: 978-1-894965-41-5

    I. Title.

PS8576.06155V43 2006   jC813'.6   C2006-901365-9

Design by hundreds & thousands design inc.

Printed in China

10 9 8 7 6 5 4 3 2 1

We gratefully acknowledge the support of the
Canada Council for the Arts and the BC Arts Council
for our publishing program.

sean moore

veggies, smeggies

The one thing in the world kids dislike the most
grows in the dirt, the lowest of lows.

They'd be outlawed if it were up to me.
I'm talking about veggies, what else could it be?

Veggies smeggies, I itch when they're mentioned —
just what were they thinking that day of invention?

"Maybe for dinner I'll have me a tree,
   with a big bowl of bushes, just nature and me!"

You may ask yourself "they" meaning just who;
who I mean is our parents, honest and for true.

Veggies smeggies, a rabbit I'm not,
but parents think different, they plan and they plot.
Thinking of schemes and dastardly deeds
to somehow convince us to eat our string beans.

No sir, not me, no peas no beans
no food should ever be that color green —
or green at all, as a matter of fact.

So from this day forward
I'm making a pact.

I'll take out the garbage,

I'll bathe without bubbles,
but I won't eat veggies.
They're nothing but trouble.

Veggies smeggies, no ma'am not today,
and say what they may, the answer is nay.
"Have one carrot, they put hair on your chest!"

I'm six years old, that wouldn't be best.

Veggies smeggies, there is never just one.

They're always in bunches,
and you can't make them fun.

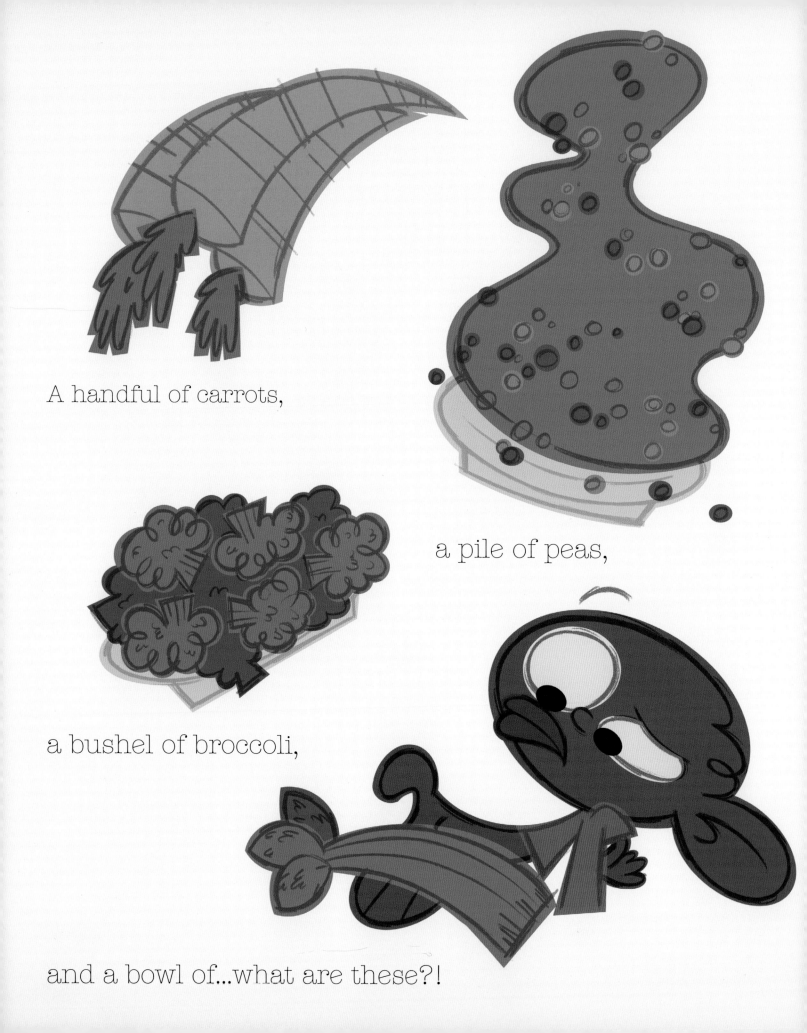

A handful of carrots,

a pile of peas,

a bushel of broccoli,

and a bowl of...what are these?!

"Well you've never tried them, just how can you tell?"
Asparagus and broccoli —
I can't even spell!

Can't spell it, won't eat it. That's my rule.
I may be young, but Mama raised no fool!

no popcorn, no pickles, or corn-on-the-cob.
It wasn't this morning that I was born,
those treat are tricks, just cucumbers and corn.

The unsolved mystery of the ripe, red tomato:
Veggie or fruit? Do you know who knows?

Well, I know they're nasty and that's all that counts.
How good could they be if they came from ground?

Veggies smeggies, more slippery than mud,
from the stem of a tomato to the roots of a spud.

My bestest friend Marc said potatoes have eyes,
and french fries aren't French, but in fact a disguise.

Well mashed or baked, not now or later.
You can cover 'em in gravy, them there are still 'taters.

Veggies smeggies: onions and eyes.
Ever wonder why they make parents cry?
It's the thought of feeding kids that filthy filth
that breaks their hearts and fills them with guilt.

Yet they still won't admit it and continue their quest,
until we're all eating grass, they simply won't rest.

Well veggies smeggies, not this time.
A child has rights and I know mine!

Calm, cool and collected, that's how I'll be —
I'll just state my case and they'll have to agree....

And please understand,
I'm not trying
to be rude.

But cabbage
and lettuce
tossed salad
and seeds?
I'm not a giraffe;
I can't live
on leaves.

Never again will
I slop on the floor,

or leave my mittens
at school anymore.

I'll go to great lengths, even tell on my friends.
I'll do anything to never eat veggies again!

"Veggies smeggies," I used to say.
I wouldn't eat one, no-how and no-way.
But I was young and foolish then,
until Grandma's tale of Uncle Ben.

Your Uncle Ben would eat to his heart's content.
Every crumb, big or small, was a dime well-spent.
But veggies smeggies, "No thank-you, please.
I would rather be stung by buzzillion bees!"

Now sure, it may seem a little extreme,

with the buzzing, the stinging, and ointment cream.
That was just how much he disliked them, you see —
where veggies were not is where Ben would be.

Unfortunate for Ben and
his jabberin' jaw,
a swarm of bees overheard
this and saw.

For outside Ben's window —
up high in a tree —
hung the home of exactly
buzzillion bees.

"Exactly how many is buzzillion?" you ask.

Well, Ben started counting, but could never keep track. "Those bees chased your uncle right out of town."

"No one has heard from him since, not even a sound."

When my grandma told me that story, we agreed
no more "veggies smeggies," from me.

We shook hands, raised our glasses, and made a deal.

What is that....

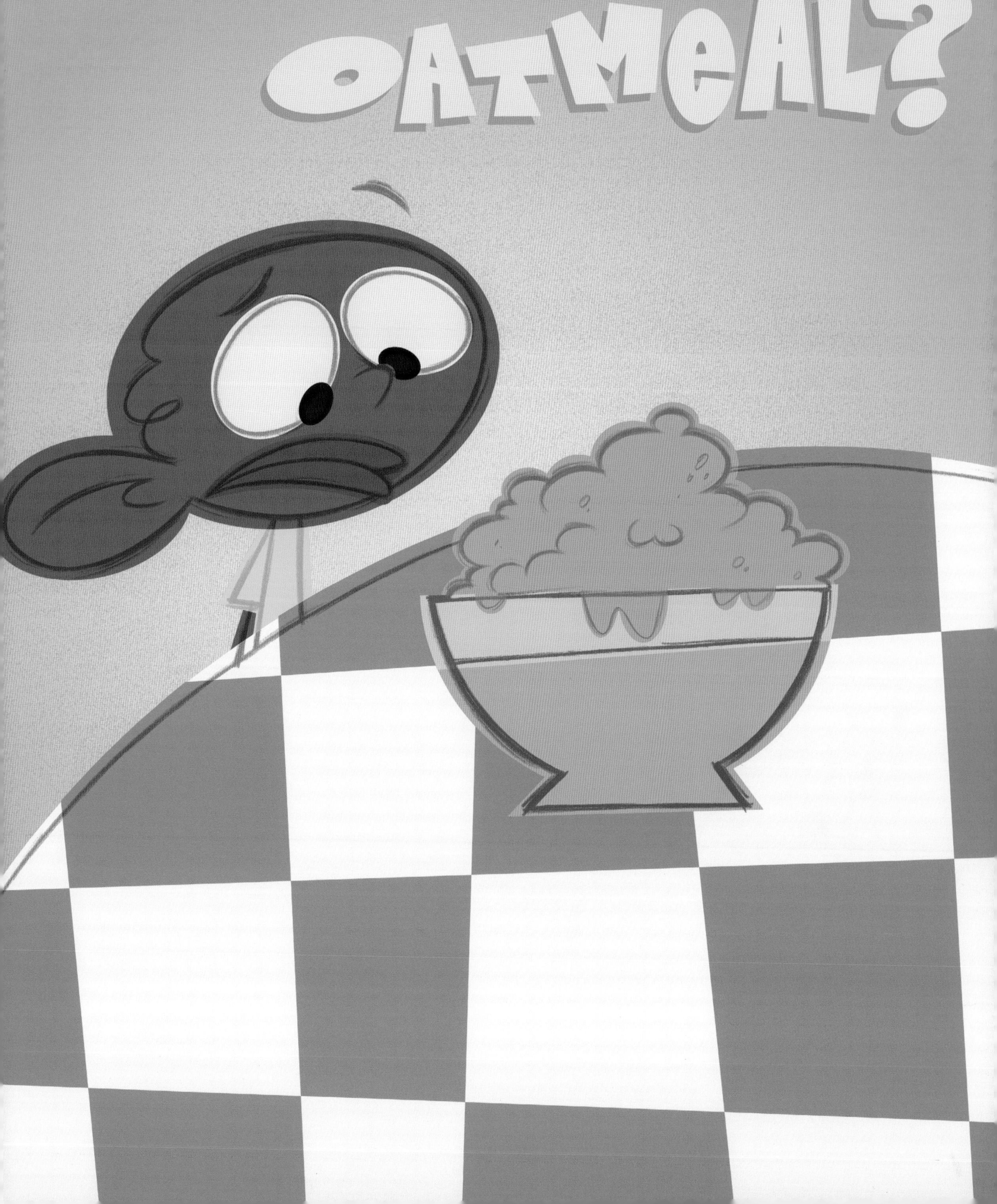